P9-ELW-302

TJ Zaps the One-Upper

Stopping One-Upping and Cell Phone Bullying

written by
Lisa Mullarkey

illustrated by
Gary LaCoste

visit us at www.abdopublishing.com

To the kids who are part of the solution...not the problem. —LM
For Ashley —GL

Published by Magic Wagon, a division of the ABDO Group, PO Box 398166, Minneapolis, MN 55439.

Printed in the United States of America, North Mankato, Minnesota.
052012
092012
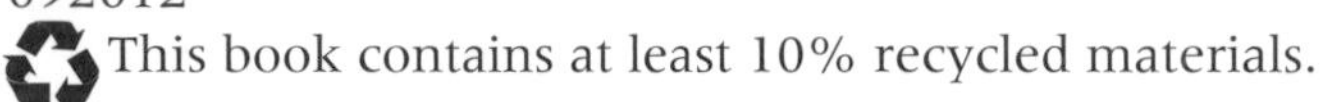
This book contains at least 10% recycled materials.

Text by Lisa Mullarkey
Illustrations by Gary LaCoste
Edited by Stephanie Hedlund and Rochelle Baltzer
Cover and interior design by Neil Klinepier

Library of Congress Cataloging-in-Publication Data
Mullarkey, Lisa.
TJ zaps the one-upper : stopping one-upping and cell phone bullying / by Lisa Mullarkey ; illustrated by Gary LaCoste.
p. cm. -- (TJ Trapper, bully zapper ; bk. 2)
Summary: TJ's former best friend, Danny, has just returned from London, but TJ finds that he has changed--he is constantly one-upping everybody, and when he uses his cell phone to send an embarrassing picture of TJ to other kids Danny takes it one step too far.
ISBN 978-1-61641-906-6
1. Bullying--Juvenile fiction. 2. Best friends--Juvenile fiction. 3. Friendship--Juvenile fiction. 4. Cell phone etiquette--Juvenile fiction. [1. Bullies--Fiction. 2. Best friends--Fiction. 3. Friendship--Fiction. 4. Cell phone etiquette--Fiction.] I. LaCoste, Gary, ill. II. Title.
PZ7.M91148Tjq 2012
813.6--dc23 2012008063

Contents

MVP

Today was *The Day*. The day I had spent two years waiting for. My neighbor and best friend was moving back from London. I woke up at five o'clock in the morning and parked myself in front of the window. Every thirty seconds I peeked through the blinds to see if the moving van had arrived.

"You could be waiting for hours, TJ," Dad said.

After waiting two years, what difference will a few more hours make? I thought.

At eleven o'clock, I saw him. "Danny's back!"

"Then let's go," chuckled Dad. He picked up a wicker basket. "We're on official welcome duty." He plopped the basket in my arms. "This will help the Greenburgs settle in." He pulled the blinds up and spoke with a James Bond accent, "Why spy when you can say 'hi'?"

I scanned the basket Auntie Stella had made for them. Toothpaste, tissues, tea bags, toilet paper . . . Whoa! "Toilet paper?" I shoved the basket back into his hands. "I'm not bringing toilet paper."

Dad laughed. "*Everyone* uses toilet paper."

I folded my arms. "Then *you* bring it."

"*Someone* better bring it!" shouted Auntie Stella. Then she added, "*If* you know what's good for you!"

Auntie Stella isn't my real aunt. But she's been helping my dad take care of me ever since I was born. Dad always says we can't live without her and she can't live without us. I think he's right.

"The boss has spoken," said Dad. He covered the toilet paper with the tissue box. "Ready?"

I was ready two years ago!

Danny pounced on me the second I walked in his garage. "Long time, no see!"

I stared at Danny. He looked . . . old. And pimply. And tall. I didn't even come up to his shoulder.

"Yep," I said. "It's been two years."

Dad put his arm around my shoulder. "TJ's excited you're back. He hardly slept last night."

My face burned. I had to think fast. I snatched the basket from Dad. "Here's some toilet paper."

Now Danny's face turned red. "Thanks . . . I guess."

While Dad talked to Danny's parents, I glanced around the garage. "Hey," I said, pointing to his bike, "I have the same one."

Danny made a duh face. "That's my *old* bike." He pointed to a sleek black-and-silver mountain bike near the window. "*That's* my new one."

"A King Cobra?" I walked over to get a closer look. "You're *so* lucky." The King Cobra was on my Christmas list. Again.

Danny dropped the basket onto a shelf. "Want to ride it? It cost 400 bucks."

"Maybe later," I said as I ran my hand over the seat.

Danny leaned on my shoulder. "I'm not sure your feet would reach the pedals anyway," he said as he slapped my back and laughed.

"Ha, ha," I said.

Danny laughed even louder. "I thought it was funny." Then he tossed me a basketball. "You still playing?"

But before I could answer, he said, "You're looking at the star of my basketball team. I made the fifth grade travel team last year." Then he pretended to shoot a basket. "You're too young for travel, aren't you? You're in what . . . fourth grade?"

Danny was a year older than me but two grades ahead. I nodded. "But last year I was voted MVP for the Hornets."

Danny didn't look impressed. "I remember the *first* time I was voted MVP." He ran his fingers through his hair. "Of course, it felt even better the *second* time. I led the league in rebounds *and* scoring." He twirled the ball on his index finger. "I averaged seventeen points a game. I haven't missed a free throw in a game in two years. You know, twenty-four months."

My nine-point average suddenly made me feel like a second-string player.

Dad chimed in. "TJ's one of the highest scorers on his team. Aren't you, TJ?"

I rolled my eyes and shifted my feet. "Not really." Then I bit my lip. "I don't think so."

"Sure you are, bud," said Dad, beaming. "He even starts now."

"Now?" said Danny. "Man, I'd flip out if I was a benchwarmer."

I glared at Danny. "I wasn't a benchwarmer."

"Whatever," he said. "At least you're a starter . . . now. That's good—for a fourth grader."

He spun the ball faster. And faster. It made me dizzy.

"So, what's your average?" asked Danny.

Mr. Greenburg looked tired. "Pace yourself, Danny. Don't wear TJ out. How about unpacking?"

Dad cleared his throat. "TJ can help for an hour. Can't you, buddy?"

Before I answered, Danny grabbed my arm and pulled me inside. "Thanks, shrimpo." He threw his head back and snorted. "Haven't you grown *at all* since I left?"

This was going to be a loooonnnnng hour.

Danny led me through a maze of boxes until we got to his room.

"Do you still read comic books?" I asked.

His dad used to drive us to Cosmic Comix to buy them every Saturday morning. I announced, "I have every Miniature Man written in the last two years. I even bought you the collector's edition in case they didn't sell it in London."

"Really?" said Danny. "Thanks. But I haven't read one since I left. Isn't Miniature Man for . . . you know . . . little kids?"

I suddenly felt smaller than Miniature Man.

The next hour went pretty much the same way. When I mentioned that Dan Gutman was my favorite author, Danny said Gutman was *his* favorite author, too. Not only had he *read* all his books, he had three of them autographed.

Even telling him about my family's trip to the Little League World Series didn't impress him. He flashed his ticket stub for Game Five of the Yankees vs. Red Sox series in my face.

During those sixty minutes, I learned something new about Danny. He had changed. A lot. He was a one-upper.

But I learned something even more important about myself. I *hate* one-uppers. Especially when they're one-upping me.

Chef TJ

When it was time to leave, I bolted to the door. "Auntie Stella's inviting your family to dinner soon."

"Good!" said Danny. "We've been eating pizza for weeks. My parents don't like to cook."

"Bobby Flay isn't your personal chef?" I asked under my breath.

"Who?" said Danny.

"What about Rachael Ray?" I asked.

Danny shrugged.

Was he kidding? Bobby Flay and Rachael Ray rocked. Auntie Stella and I loved to watch the Food Network. I even entered their Kids Cook-Off Contest.

An Iron Chef moment simmered in my head. "Come tonight. I'll cook for you!"

I flashed him my biggest smile. There was *no way* Danny could one-up me in the kitchen.

"Tonight?" asked Auntie Stella when I rushed home and told her.

I held up a package of chicken. "It's good practice for the contest. I want to win."

Auntie Stella hugged me. "You're already a winner to me. But if you promise to wash and dry the dishes, it's a deal."

"Deal," I said. "We'll have chicken with garlic smashed potatoes."

Auntie Stella laughed. "What a surprise! I think we've perfected the recipe, TJ. I can smell victory! Taste victory!" Then she scratched her head. "What about dessert?"

"Your chocolate bowls with ice cream, of course," I said. "Danny will love them."

When the Greenburgs arrived, Danny headed straight for the TV. "Nice TV. Is it 3-D? Ours is."

Of course it was.

Dad smiled. "Nope. No fancy TVs here. We don't watch it that much."

Danny's mouth fell open. "Really?"

"This is the only one we have," said Dad.

Danny's eyes widened. "We have six in our house. Six."

Of course he did.

Five minutes later Auntie Stella announced, "Dinner's served."

"Delish!" said Mrs. Greenburg after she took a bite. "You'll have to share your recipe, Stella."

"It's TJ's special recipe," said Auntie Stella. "My lips are sealed."

Danny stuffed his mouth with chicken then yawned. "What's there to do in this town now?"

I thought for a minute. "We play baseball or basketball."

"The library has a reading program," said Dad. "With prizes."

"TJ won a prize last year," said Auntie Stella.

Danny perked up. "I won the *grand* prize in my summer reading contest."

Of course he did. The one-upper strikes again!

A minute later, Auntie Stella spoke up. "Ethan and TJ signed up for the Mad Scientist Strikes Back Camp at the library. It starts in a couple of weeks. Maybe there's a spot left for you."

Before I could say a word, Danny bobbed his head up and down. "Science is my favorite subject. I get straight As."

Of course he did.

Then he asked, "Who's Ethan?"

When I told him, he looked about as interested as a boy at a ballet recital. Instead, he started rattling off all the times he made honor roll.

So while Danny bragged about his grades, Auntie Stella and I headed into the kitchen to make dessert.

While Auntie Stella melted the chocolate, I blew up the balloons. Ten minutes later, twelve chocolate-covered balloons sat on cookie sheets.

"Now *those* look interesting," said Mrs. Greenburg as she and Danny piled dishes into the sink.

TJ's Chocolate Paradise

1. Blow up some balloons to about the size of a softball.
2. With an adult's help, melt chunks of milk chocolate in a saucepan. Stir. When melted, let the chocolate cool for a little bit.
3. Swirl the bottom half of the balloons in the chocolate. Set the chocolate-covered balloons on wax paper to cool.
4. Once the chocolate hardens, carefully pop the balloons. Peel the balloon away from the "bowl."
5. Fill the bowls with whatever floats your boat.

As everyone crowded around, I imagined myself accepting the grand prize in the Food Network contest. A gold measuring cup hung around my neck. Bobby Flay was handing me a check for $10,000. I was about to thank Auntie Stella for her help when my daydream suddenly ended.

I heard a small *pfff*. Then *POP! POP! POP!* I spun around in time to see my neat rows of balloons exploding one after another. Chocolate shards flew everywhere.

Mrs. Greenburg looked like she had a case of cocoa pox. Danny's arms were splattered with flecks of brown gunk. Auntie Stella's white sweater was now a chocolate tie-dyed mess.

"The chocolate was too hot!" said Dad.

And just like that, dinner was over. Without dessert.

When Mr. and Mrs. Greenburg left, Danny stayed behind to watch me chisel chocolate off of the counters and walls.

"So, what's your secret ingredient in the chicken?" Danny asked.

I bit my lip. "I'm not telling."

"What's the big deal?" said Danny.

I shrugged. "It's top secret."

Danny rolled his eyes and begged me for the recipe.

I wanted Danny to shut up and go home. Chocolate was up my nose, in my ears, and caked on my hair. It must have invaded my brain cells because before I knew it, I blurted out, "Crushed pistachios." Then I threw the recipe cards at him.

Danny scanned the cards and smirked. "Since you told me your secret, want to know my free throw secret?"

I bobbed my head up and down. "Yes!"

"I'm sure you would!" he yelled. Then, he bolted out the door, leaving behind smudgy brown footprints.

That's when I officially declared Danny Greenburg a one-upper *and* a full-fledged jerk.

"Danny's gone?" asked Dad a few minutes later.

"I don't like him anymore," I mumbled. "He's changed."

"Give him a chance, TJ." Dad flicked a stray piece of chocolate off my shirt. "Maybe you'll be on the same basketball team this year. Did you know he plays point guard?"

My stomach did a layup. Then it sunk to my feet. At that moment, I wanted to slam dunk Danny.

"Point guard's my position," I said. "There's only room for one of them on the court and you're looking at him." I

chugged a bottle of water. Then I tossed it into the recycling can fifteen feet away.

"Swish." I burped. "Three points. Let's see Danny do that."

King Cobra Strikes Again

"Salutations," said Livvy on the school playground the next morning. "Did everyone have a good weekend?"

I grumbled. "Not really." I kicked a stone across the playground. "Unless you think it's fun to be one-upped a million times."

Ethan looked confused. "Did Danny move back yet?" He turned to Livvy and

Maxi. "Danny is TJ's best friend. His dad was transferred to London a few years ago but he's back now."

I sighed. "Danny *was* my best friend. He's not anymore."

Ethan looked surprised. "Really? What happened?"

"He's a one-upper," I said. "Everything he has is better than mine. Bigger than mine. Costs more than mine."

Livvy laughed. "So I'm not the new kid anymore!"

I patted her on the back. "Sorry. You're still the new kid here. Danny doesn't go to our school. He goes to St. Michael's. And he's older than us. He's in sixth grade."

"At least you don't have to see him in school," said Maxi. "He can't one-up you here."

Maxi was right! I felt a little bit better.

Ethan took a baseball out of his backpack. "Are we still playing at Randall Park after school?"

We played baseball every Monday at Randall Park. "Yep." Then I thought of Danny again. Randall Park was right next to St. Michael's School. I crossed my fingers that Danny would be home way before we got to the park.

My finger crossing didn't work. I wasn't even there for five minutes when he showed up just as we were about to pick teams.

He squatted behind the fence with his hands shoved in his pockets. I adjusted my cap and pretended not to see him.

Danny coughed.

I ignored him.

He coughed again. A few kids glanced his way. I didn't.

By the time I finally looked over, Danny was sitting on his King Cobra eating a candy bar. The whole dessert fiasco popped into my head. The last thing I needed was for him to blab about it. *Pedal away, Danny. Fast.*

No such luck. He jumped off his bike and sat in the dugout. If my Auntie Stella saw him, she'd say he looked like he lost his best friend. I tried to ignore him some more. But after a few minutes and more coughing, I waved him over. He trotted toward the mound with a goofy grin on his face.

"Wanna play?" I asked.

He nodded. "I'm in."

"You're first, TJ," said Niko, a fifth grader. "Pick."

Danny inched toward me. Was he serious? I always picked Ethan first. *Always.*

"Ethan," I said as we chest bumped.

When it was Niko's turn, Danny stepped back and dug his sneaker into the dirt. He created a mini dust cloud.

Before my next pick, I spied Bling Bling Bryce walking into the dugout. Bling Bling was a sixth grader like Danny. Thanks to his father's jewelry store, Bling Bling had more gold than the stash found in King Tut's tomb.

Bling Bling always cracked me up. I didn't care if he ran as slow as a tortoise, I always picked him for my team.

"You playin', Bling Bling?" I called to him.

He untangled a strand of hair from a necklace. "Yep."

"Bling Bling's mine," I said.

Bling Bling jingled toward me.

Danny gave me the evil eye.

Then Niko picked Lamar.

We went on picking for five more rounds. Finally, Danny put his hands together in front of his chest and mouthed "Please?"

He reminded me of a puppy waiting to be adopted from the pound. I caved. "Danny."

Danny pumped his hand in the air and trotted over to Bling Bling. "How can you run with all those necklaces on?"

"Chains," said Bling Bling. "Necklaces are for girls."

Danny pointed to the diamond stud in Bling Bling's ear. "Nice earring. My mom has diamonds twice the size."

Ethan shot me a look and whispered, "Is he one-upping Bling Bling?"

I shrugged. *Better him than me.*

Twenty minutes later, Danny smacked a three-run homer over the center field fence. Then he hit a triple and turned a double play. The kid was good at *everything*.

Me? I banged out a double, struck out three times, and dropped a fly ball. Twice.

"At least I got a double," I said to Ethan as I hopped on my bike.

"I got a home run *and* a triple," beamed Danny. Then he jumped on his bike and smirked. "Wanna race? My King Cobra is *way* faster than your bike."

I suddenly wanted to slither away.

Caught Red-handed

"How was baseball?" asked Auntie Stella when I got home.

"We won," I said. "But it wasn't because of me. I had a terrible game." I grabbed a water bottle out of the fridge. "It was the worst game of my life. I struck out *three* times."

I chugged the entire bottle. "I'm going to be picked last tomorrow. I just know it." I slid out a chair and plopped down in it. "But Danny . . ."

Auntie Stella looked surprised. "Danny was there?" she asked as she sliced veggies. "That's nice, isn't it?"

"Nice?" I said. "No way, Auntie Stella. It was *awful*." I snatched a piece of pepper from the cutting board. "Can I tell you something?"

She wiped her hands on her apron and pulled out a chair. "This sounds serious. You know you can tell me anything." She sat down. "Spill it."

"I *hate* Danny Greenburg. He's *constantly* one-upping me. He brags that his bike is better. His TV is better. His grades are better. He's only been back three days, but I'm already sick of him."

I pounded my fist on the table. "Oh, and did I mention that while I was busy striking out, Danny smacked a three-run homer over the center field fence? Center field! Then he hit a triple and turned a double play."

I took a deep breath. "Yep, I hate that kid."

Auntie Stella patted my back. "Hate is a strong word. I hate brussels sprouts. I hate when I burn my cookies. And I hate when I can't solve the puzzle on *Wheel of Fortune*. But I don't hate *people*. Dislike some people? Yes." She pushed another pepper slice toward me. "But I understand how you feel."

"You do?" I asked. "Really?"

She nodded. "I had a friend who one-upped me in college." She twirled her dish towel in the air. "I wanted to give her the old dish towel." *Snap!* "Once she started spreading rumors about me, I ditched her. Does Danny make you feel bad? Because she sure tried to make me feel bad."

Just then, Danny poked his head in the back door. "Hey, TJ. Want to shoot some hoops? I brought my basketball since yours needs air. Mine bounces twice as high, you know."

Of course it does.

Auntie Stella smiled and patted my arm. Then she popped out of her chair. "Hi, Danny. Want a pepper? It's a hot one."

"I can't eat that kind," said Danny. "One bite and my eyes start to tear up."

Auntie Stella's eyes lit up. "Really? TJ here can eat *five* of them. At a time. Without water."

I could? That was news to me! I gave Auntie Stella a strange look.

"No way! Really?" said Danny. "You should enter one of those food-eating contests. I once saw a kid eat twelve hot dogs in fifteen minutes."

"Only twelve?" said Auntie Stella. "TJ's eaten *thirteen* hot dogs in fifteen minutes." She winked at me.

Auntie Stella was helping me one-up Danny! "It was *fourteen,* Auntie Stella. Not thirteen."

"That's almost a hot dog a minute!" said Danny. Then he pointed outside. "Let's play some b-ball, TJ. I broke my record yesterday. I made forty-eight out of fifty free throws in a row."

"That's great," said Auntie Stella. "You made *almost* as many as TJ. He made forty-nine out of fifty last week. Right, TJ?"

"Yep," I said. "The last one circled the rim but didn't go in." This one-upping was starting to feel really, really good!

But the feeling didn't last very long. I heard shuffling behind me. Then a hand squeezed my shoulder. "Really, TJ? Why didn't you tell me about that? Making forty-nine out of fifty baskets is amazing."

I sunk down in my chair. *Dad!*

Then Dad turned to Auntie Stella. "I never knew TJ liked hot dogs so much. You two sure keep a lot of secrets from me."

Auntie Stella's face turned as red as the tomato she was slicing. She looked at her watch. "My, my. Look at the time. I better get back to dinner."

"And I have homework, Danny," I said. "Sorry."

When Danny left, Dad poured himself a glass of water. "Okay, you two. You're busted. What exactly were you up to?"

Auntie Stella shook her finger in the air. "Danny's been one-upping TJ ever since he moved back to town." She patted my shoulder. "So I just gave him a little taste of his own medicine."

"He's eleven, Stella," said Dad. "You stooped down to his level?"

Auntie Stella straightened her apron and lowered her eyes. "Well, I just hated to see TJ upset."

"So you lied and told Danny that TJ eats peppers and hot dogs? That's absurd."

Auntie Stella was about to say something but snapped her mouth shut.

"Sorry, Dad," I sighed. "I just couldn't take it anymore. Danny's been one-upping me to death. He's been home three days, but I'm ready for him to go back to London."

"And you, Stella?" said Dad.

She scrunched her nose and flicked a towel through the air. "I should have snapped him with my dish towel instead."

Dad raised his eyebrows and tried to hold back a smile. "Give him a break, people. He just moved back. He has to make new friends. Try out for teams again. Meet new teachers and go to a different school. I'm sure he's just trying to find his way."

I shook my head. "He's showing off all of the time. He's one-upping me every chance he gets."

"Talk to him about it," said Dad. "He may not even know he's doing it."

Talk to Danny? Was he serious?

I'd rather help him pack.

A Slam Dunk

During school the next day, an announcement came over the loudspeaker. "Basketball tryouts for boys in grades four through six will be held tonight. Tryouts for the girls are a week from today. Good luck to all."

"Who's trying out?" asked Livvy. "I am!"

"Really?" asked Maxi. "No kidding?"

"How hard can it be?" asked Livvy. "You throw a little ball into a big basket.

You get five points each time you make it. Right?"

I tried not to laugh. "No, Livvy. Each basket is worth two points. And making that basket is harder than you think."

Maxi pretended to shoot a basket. "I wanted to try out, but someone told me I'm too short."

Ethan and I stared at Livvy.

She raised her hands up in the air. "It wasn't me! I'm a changed lady!" Then she crossed her heart. "Honest to goodness I am."

When Livvy came to our class earlier in the year, she was a bully. She would call people names and pick on them but then say *just kidding*. With the help of me, TJ Trapper, Bully Zapper, she's working hard to stop bullying.

Maxi laughed. "It wasn't Livvy. It was my cousin. She was on the team last year."

Livvy put her arm around Maxi's shoulder. "Maxi, Ms. Perry says you never know until you try. So you have to try. You're a fast runner. I bet you could run around those players and get 100 points all by yourself."

Maxi jumped up and down. "Really? I'll try out if you try out."

So while Livvy and Maxi talked about their tryouts, Ethan and I talked about ours.

"Any other point guards trying out?" asked Ethan.

Danny's face flashed in my mind. "Danny plays point," I told Ethan. "But I'm not sure if he's trying out. He doesn't go to our school."

Maxi said, "My cousin Sarah goes to St. Michael's. She was on the team here last year."

I groaned. "Danny's probably going to make it and be our point guard."

"I used to be a cheerleader," said Livvy. "Want me to come and cheer you on? Then you and Ethan can be our cheerleaders next week."

"Thanks," I said. "But I don't think Coach Daltry wants cheerleaders at tryouts."

"Don't worry," Ethan said to me. "You'll make the team."

But I wasn't so sure.

"Ready to go?" asked Dad after dinner. "Practice starts in twenty minutes."

"Ready," I said as I grabbed a water bottle.

When we went outside, Danny was waiting by our car. "What are you doing?"

He threw me his basketball. "You're dad offered me a ride. Are you ready for tryouts?"

I took a deep breath. "Guess so. I have on my lucky shirt."

Danny looked me up and down. "I have on my lucky shirt *and* my lucky shorts."

Of course he did.

"Did you bring water, boys?" said Dad. "You'll be thirsty."

I held up my water. "I brought a bottle."

"One bottle?" asked Danny. "I brought two."

Of course he did.

"You might want to go back and get another," said Danny.

I ignored him and climbed into the car. Danny bragged about his travel team the whole car ride. "I'll show you my trophies the next time you come over."

I can't wait.

When my dad dropped us off, he yelled out the window, "Good luck, boys!"

As Danny slammed the door, I heard him mumble, "He's going to need it."

I wanted to prove Danny wrong. And I did for the first half of tryouts. I sunk most of my shots and nailed my first three-pointer.

"Nice," said Coach Daltry as he wrote something on his clipboard. "Let's see you shoot some foul shots."

I walked up to the line and sunk ten out of ten. Ethan gave me a high five.

"Next," said Coach Daltry.

Danny walked up to the line and stood there for a second before sinking the first one.

"All net," said Coach Daltry. "Show me nine more just like it."

But Danny couldn't do it. He missed every other one. He shrugged and walked over to get some water.

By the time Coach Daltry told us to take a break, I had scored twenty-three points and had six assists.

I chugged my water and sat next to Danny. "I shot two three-pointers."

Danny wiped the sweat off of his face. "Big deal."

It was a big deal. To me. But I didn't want to brag. "I guess I'm just lucky tonight."

But my luck didn't last long. During the second half, Danny scored thirty points, blocked four of my shots, and landed on my foot after one of his jump shots.

"My ankle!" I screamed, glaring at Danny. "You landed on my foot."

Coach Daltry helped me up. "Accidents happen, TJ."

Two days later during our first practice game, I sat on the bench with a swollen ankle while Danny started as point guard.

Another slam dunk for Danny.

Cell Phone Bully

By the time science camp rolled around, Danny knew half the kids in town. Everyone seemed to like him. The kids at camp? Yep. The basketball team? Check. The guys at the field? You betcha!

Danny zapped the fun out of science camp when he declared himself Danny Nye the Science Guy. He bragged he knew everything about a chronometer, pyrometer, and densimeter. The only meter I knew was my Annoy-O-Meter, thanks to him. When we made papier-mâché models of the planets, Danny spilled the beans and told everyone about the Great Chocolate Fiasco.

"They didn't explode," I said. "Not really . . ."

"Oh, yes, they did," said Danny. "There was chocolate everywhere. Even on his underwear."

Everyone laughed.

"He's lying," I said. But no one was listening to me. Most kids were checking their cell phones.

Danny pointed to his phone. "Here's the proof."

Everyone who had a cell phone started to laugh. When I grabbed Niko's phone to see what was so funny, I saw a picture of me covered with chocolate gunk. It was in my hair, on my shirt, and in my nose. If you looked real close, you could see my underwear sticking out of my pants with smudgy chocolate goo! My face felt like it was on fire.

Then Danny used his phone to take a picture of me and my red face! He pounded the table with his fist and laughed. "You look like a pig in this picture. Your nostrils are flared." Then he started to snort and oink.

"Don't send that picture to anyone," I warned.

The room filled up with cell phone beeps. "Too late," Danny snorted.

Livvy took out her phone. She was the only fourth grader with one. "Don't worry, TJ, I'm deleting it. Danny's being a bully."

Then Ethan spoke up. "If I had a phone, I'd delete it, too. Everyone should delete the pictures."

A fifth grade girl raised her phone in the air. "Deleted." She turned to Danny. "I don't know how you got my number but if you ever text me again, I'll tell my mom."

Danny didn't look like he cared until the camp counselor walked up behind him and grabbed his phone. "Unacceptable," she said. "You've lost this phone until your parents come in for a little chat. Understand?"

Danny nodded. "Sorry, TJ." He lowered his head. "I really am. I acted like a jerk."

I believed him. At least until I got on the bus the next day and heard a bunch of kids snorting like a pig. When Ms. Perry asked why some kids in the hall were snorting when they walked by me, Ethan told her all about Danny Greenburg.

"I'm not tattling," said Ethan.

She nodded. "I know, Ethan. You're reporting and it's very brave of you to do that. TJ's being bullied." She whipped out her notebook and wrote something down. "Have you told your dad, TJ?"

I shook my head. "He's good friends with Danny's parents. And it's only been a few days."

"One day of bullying is one day too many," said Ms. Perry. "And sending pictures through texts is unacceptable. I'm going to call the principal over at St. Michael's."

"Can I talk to my dad first?" I said. "Maybe we can solve the problem tonight."

Ms. Perry agreed. "Have your dad call me first thing in the morning. I want to make sure Danny knows he's being a bully and stop it before it gets worse."

When I got home, Auntie Stella was on the phone. While I ate a snack, I flipped through the newspaper looking for the food section. I almost choked on my cookie when I saw a recipe for *Perfect Pistachio Chicken*. Skimming the list of ingredients, it looked exactly like *my* recipe for Pistachio Chicken. It couldn't be!

My eyes jumped to the bottom of the page. I saw something that made my heart beat faster than my turbo-charged electric mixer: *Submitted by Danny Greenburg, Age 11.* DANNY GREENBURG?

Six months of cracking pistachio shells and eating pounds and pounds of chicken were wasted. It was like Danny ripped out my guts and blenderized them.

I grabbed the paper and stomped over to the Greenburgs' house. I banged on the door and flapped the newspaper under Danny's nose when he answered.

"Why would you do this?" I demanded.

He grabbed the paper. "Hey! They printed it. How cool is that?"

Cool? He thought it was cool to steal my recipe? "You've ruined everything, Danny. Everything," I repeated.

Danny's smile faded. "I thought you'd be happy to get your recipe in the paper."

"You thought wrong. Now *everyone* knows my secret ingredient. I can't enter it in the contest now. The rules said it had to be an *unpublished* recipe." I threw the paper to the ground. "Plus, no one knows it's *my* recipe, since *you* took credit for it. It took me six months to perfect that recipe and just one day for you to ruin it."

Danny scooped up the paper. "I didn't know you'd be this upset. It was a joke."

My knees shook. My eye twitched. I turned away and stomped back home.

When I got there, I told Auntie Stella everything.

She put her hands on her cheeks. "How awful! I'd be upset, too, TJ. You worked so hard on that recipe."

And when Dad found out, he was steaming mad. Mad enough to go over to the Greenburgs' house.

Even though I had a headache, I felt a tiny bit better that he *finally* saw the real Danny. What took him so long?

While we waited for my dad to get back, Auntie Stella tried to cheer me up. She slid scrambled eggs, bacon, and sausage onto my plate. "Since you love breakfast for dinner, I whipped up your favorites."

As I shoveled the eggs into my mouth, I could only think of one thing: I wanted to scramble up Danny Greenburg.

Poor Sportsmanship

"What did Danny say?" asked Auntie Stella when Dad got home. "Is he sorry?"

"He better be sorry," I said. "Are his parents mad?"

Dad ran his fingers through his hair. He slowly shook his head. Then he shrugged. "I'm almost speechless."

Auntie Stella pulled out a chair and patted the cushion. I sat down. "What happened?" I asked.

Dad was still shaking his head. Then he rubbed his head like he had a headache.

"I confronted Danny about the recipe," said Dad. "He admitted it right away. His parents were upset. In fact, they looked really disappointed in Danny. They said he'd be grounded."

"That sounds promising," said Auntie Stella. "The Greenburgs *will* punish Danny. I just know it."

Dad squished his face. "I wouldn't bet on it, Stella. Because when I told them about the one-upping and the cell phone pictures, they didn't seem concerned at all."

"What do you mean?" said Auntie Stella. "They didn't care?"

"They said that boys will be boys," said Dad. "Mr. Greenburg said it was a harmless prank. It was *only* a few pictures."

Auntie Stella picked up her dish towel and started to walk toward the door. "Stella!" said Dad as he tugged on her apron and pulled her back toward the table. "Stay here."

"I want to give them a piece of my mind," said Auntie Stella. "They need to know that Danny can't bully TJ."

"I explained that it had to stop," said Dad. "I let them know if it doesn't, I'll have to report it. That is if TJ's teacher doesn't beat me to it."

"Ms. Perry said she's going to call his principal," I said. "He's going to be in a lot of trouble."

Dad smiled. "Ms. Perry seems to be on top of it. That's good to know, TJ."

Then his smile disappeared. "But what really troubles me," said Dad, "is that Danny and his parents don't think it's a big deal. But it *is* a big deal. Our school district has zero tolerance for bullies. I'm pretty sure his school does as well."

"What should I do now?" I asked. "He's probably really mad at me."

Auntie Stella sighed. "He should be mad at himself. And embarrassed! That's what he should be. Not to mention sorry!"

Dad chewed on his lip. I could tell he was thinking up a plan. "I'm going to drive you to school tomorrow. And then Ms. Perry and I will call his principal. Maybe she can get through to the Greenburgs that 'kids will be kids' isn't acceptable anymore. Times have changed since they moved away. There are new rules. And some new laws."

Auntie Stella waved her hands in the air. "Let's forget about Danny for the rest of the night." She grabbed her recipe book. "I think we need to enter another recipe in the contest. You make a mean taco, TJ!"

"Not tonight, Auntie Stella," I said. "If you don't mind, I just want to go to my room. I'm not feeling that great."

Auntie Stella and Dad raised their eyebrows. But before they could say anything else, I ran up the stairs.

I didn't see Danny again until basketball practice the next night.

When Dad dropped Ethan and me off, he said, "I'm going to hang out and watch. I want to be sure everything's okay."

"Did he get in trouble at school?" asked Ethan.

Dad shrugged. "Wish I could fill you in, Ethan. But I can't. It's considered confidential even though it involves you."

"Me?" asked Ethan in a surprised voice.

Dad nodded. "TJ said you were an upstander. You and Livvy told the kids to delete the pictures. If we had more upstanders like you, we'd have less bullying."

"It wasn't a big deal," said Ethan. "I was just sticking up for TJ."

I grabbed my bag and opened the door. "It was a big deal to me, Ethan. Thanks!" When I shut the door, I saw Danny walking into the gym.

"Don't worry," said Dad. "I'm here." Then he pointed to Ethan. "Ethan has your back, too."

During practice, Danny acted like nothing happened. "Nice shot," he said when I made a jump shot.

When I ran out of water, he tossed me one of his extra bottles.

And when I made ten foul shots in a row, he gave me a high five.

"Maybe he got in a lot of trouble," said Ethan when practice ended. "Maybe his parents punished him for the rest of the year."

"Maybe he learned a lesson," I said as I pushed open the door to the locker room.

That's when I knew he hadn't learned anything at all. Because plastered on a dozen lockers were pictures of me in Auntie Stella's apron. *This Little Piggy Baked a Cake!* was written on each picture.

Before I could tear them down, the rest of the team burst through the door. Danny led the way and started snorting. A few kids laughed until Coach Daltry walked in after the last kid.

SNORT SNORT
THIS LITTLE PIGGY
BAKED A CAKE!
THIS LITTLE PIGGY
BAKED A CAKE!
THIS LITTLE PIGGY
BAKED A CAKE!
THIS LITTLE PIGGY
BAKED A CAKE!
THIS LITTLE PIGGY
BAKED A CAKE!
THIS LITTLE PIGGY
BAKED A CAKE!

He snatched one of the pictures off of a locker and waved it in the air. "Who took this picture? Who hung them up?"

Danny snorted. "That would be me, Coach. Isn't it funny?"

Coach crumpled the paper in his hand. "Funny?" Then he pulled Danny's pledge of Good Sportsmanship out of a folder. "In my office, Greenburg." He waved to the rest of us. "See everyone at practice tomorrow."

But Danny wasn't at practice the next day. Or the day after that. Or the day after that.

Danny was kicked off the team.

A New Day, A New Danny?

A few days later during free reading, Ms. Perry called me up to her desk. "How are you doing, TJ? Are you feeling okay about things?"

I jammed my hands in my pockets. "Guess so. I haven't seen Danny since he got kicked off the team."

And I didn't plan to either!

"Do you think he'll send any more pictures?" I asked. "I still have no idea when he took the picture of me and Auntie Stella baking." I covered my face with my hands. "I told Auntie Stella that I'm never wearing another apron as long as I live."

"I hope he doesn't send any more pictures," Ms. Perry said.

I groaned. "What if he finds a way to take more pictures? What if he sends them to the seventh and eighth graders next time?" My stomach hurt just thinking about it. "He could have taken them already. I told Auntie Stella that we need to keep the shades down."

Ms. Perry smiled. "Try not to worry. We're on top of it, TJ. We're monitoring the situation closely. I promise." Then she let out a deep sigh. "Danny didn't seem too concerned about his bullying behavior until Coach Daltry pulled him off the basketball team. His family wasn't happy about it. Neither was he. But his principal reminded them that it was better than being suspended from school."

"Suspended?" I asked. "Would they really do that to a sixth grader?"

"Yep," said Ms. Perry. "It doesn't matter what grade you're in. We're not tolerating bullying from anyone. We told Danny that he has to have a clean record if he wants to try out for baseball in the spring. Apparently, he really wants to play travel ball. He knows it's not going to happen unless his behavior improves."

"What should I do if he picks on me again?" I said.

"Tell an adult," said Ms. Perry. "Do what you've been doing. You're neighbors. You don't need to be best buds, but you

certainly don't want to be enemies. You'll run into him at some point."

She was right about that.

After school that day, my knees felt weak when I saw Bling Bling Bryce and Danny ride into Randall Park with their gloves.

Niko and Lamar were just starting to

pick teams. "You playing, Danny?"

Danny glanced at me and looked away quickly. "Yep. I need to practice every day if I want to make the baseball team in spring." He picked up a baseball and ran toward center field.

When it was Lamar's turn to pick, I crossed my fingers hoping he'd pick me. He didn't. I ended up on the same team as Danny.

We didn't really talk to each other, which was fine with me. I was just glad he didn't call me shrimpo or try to one-up me again.

When the game was over, Niko asked if he could borrow Danny's phone. Danny folded his arms over his chest. "My mom said I'm too young for a cell phone. She took it away yesterday. I can't get it back until . . ."

But he didn't finish his sentence.

"Until he stops bullying," whispered Ethan. "But it looks like he has."

I rolled my eyes. "This was only the first time I've seen him. I doubt he's stopped bullying. My dad says a bully never changes overnight."

"Livvy did," said Ethan. "Didn't she?"

I shrugged. "Livvy says she changed. She meets with Mrs. Morris every week. But Dad says time will tell."

"Maybe you'll get lucky with Danny, too," said Ethan. Then he groaned. "I just hope he doesn't start to bully someone else. Like me!"

"If he does," I said, "you know who you can call for help, don't you?"

"Auntie Stella and her dish towel?" said Ethan.

I laughed. "Yep. And your parents, and my dad, and Ms. Perry, and Coach Daltry, and the most important person of all . . ."

"Who?" asked Ethan

"Me," I said. "TJ Trapper, Bully Zapper."

The Bully Test

Have you ever been a bully? Ask yourself these questions.

Do I like to leave others out to make them feel bad?

Have I ever spread a rumor that I knew was not true?

Do I like teasing others?

Do I call others mean names to make myself feel better or get attention?

Is it funny to me to see other kids getting made fun of?

If you answered yes to any of these questions, it's not too late to change. First, say "I'm sorry." And start treating others the way you want to be treated.

Be a Bully Zapper

A few tips on how to stop bullying that happens around you:

Tell your friends when bullying happens and ask them to stand up for people if they hear it happening. There is power in numbers.

Report bullying to an adult you trust. This is the most important thing you can do to stop bullying.

Don't spread rumors. If you hear a rumor, don't pass it along. Stopping a rumor helps stop bullying.

Speak up for your friends. Bullies back down if they get attention they don't want.

Bullying Glossary

bystander - someone who watches but is not a part of a situation.

ignore - to not pay attention to someone or something.

one-upper - a person who always does something better than another or has something better than someone else.

reporting - telling an adult about being bullied.

rumor - talk that may not be true but is repeated by many people.

social bullying - telling secrets, spreading rumors, giving mean looks, and leaving kids out on purpose.

tattling - telling someone about another's actions in order to get him or her in trouble.

upstander - someone who sees bullying and stands up for the person being bullied.

zero tolerance - automatic punishment for bullying.

Further Reading

Fox, Debbie. *Good-Bye Bully Machine.* Minneapolis: Free Spirit Publishing, 2009.

Hall, Megan Kelley. *Dear Bully: Seventy Authors Tell Their Stories.* New York: HarperTeen, 2011.

Romain, Trevor. *Bullies Are a Pain in the Brain.* Minneapolis: Free Spirit Publishing, 1997.

Web Sites

To learn more about bullying, visit ABDO Group online. Web sites about bullying are featured on our Book Links page. These links are routinely monitored and updated to provide the most current information available. **www.abdopublishing.com**

About the Author

Lisa Mullarkey is the author of the popular chapter book series, Katharine the Almost Great. She wears many hats: mom, teacher, librarian, and author. She is passionate about children's literature. She lives in New Jersey with her husband, John, and her children, Sarah and Matthew. She's happy to report that none of them are bullies.

About the Illustrator

Gary LaCoste began his illustration career 15 years ago. His clients included Hasbro, Nickelodeon, and Lego. Lately his focus has shifted to children's publishing, where he's enjoyed illustrating more than 25 titles. Gary happily lives in western Massachusetts with his wife, Miranda, and daughter, Ashley.